Following Grandfather

Following Grandfather

Rosemary Wells

illustrated by Christopher Denise

CANDLEWICK PRESS

Text copyright © 2012 by Rosemary Wells
Illustrations copyright © 2012 by Christopher Denise

First edition 2012

Library of Congress Cataloging-in-Publication Data

Wells, Rosemary.
Following Grandfather / Rosemary Wells ; [illustrated by Christopher Denise]. — 1st ed.
p. cm.
Summary: Jenny is as close to her grandfather as a mouse can be, and when he suddenly dies, she
keeps thinking she sees him — turning a corner, sitting on a bench, heading for the pier,
or walking along their beloved beach, seeking the elusive queen's teacup seashell.
ISBN 978-0-7636-5069-8
[1. Grandfathers — Fiction. 2. Grief — Fiction. 3. Mice — Fiction. 4. Italian Americans — Fiction. 5. Boston
(Mass.) — History — 20th century — Fiction.] I. Denise, Christopher, ill. II. Title.
PZ7.W46843Fol 2012
[E] — dc23   2011048349

12 13 14 15 16 17 WOR 10 9 8 7 6 5 4 3 2 1

Printed in Stevens Point, WI, U.S.A.

This book was typeset in Cochin.
The illustrations were created digitally.

Candlewick Press
99 Dover Street
Somerville, Massachusetts 02144

visit us at www.candlewick.com

For Phoebe Snow Wells

R. W.

For Laurie

C. D.

Chapter One

Down at the very end of Revere Beach, where the people never go, the mice of Boston spread their towels and plant their beach umbrellas in the sun. Grandfather and I were among them every summer Sunday.

So were the mice who lived in the home
of Senator Henry Cabot Lodge Jr. They
were terrible snobs. They smelled of butter
pastry and they did not talk to my grandfather or me, although we usually had our
picnic not ten feet from their beach umbrella.

The Lodge bathing suits were blue with white piping. Even their umbrellas were navy blue with a big white $\mathcal{L}$ on one panel. There were always a lot of young Lodge mice running up and down the beach.

"Maybe one of them will be my friend," I said to my grandfather.

"Don't hold your breath, Jenny," answered Grandfather. "The Lodge mice, the Saltonstall mice, the Lowell mice — their ancestors all came to America in the days before George Washington, stowed away in biscuit tins. Now they're all living in those fancy brownstones on Beacon Hill." Grandfather's silver whiskers stood up at angles from his face, and his fine Roman nose quivered.

Grandfather opened a beautiful clam with his pocketknife and set it on the coals of a driftwood fire to cook. Grandfather found the clams just below the tide line,

where they squirted up in the wet sand. The clams were pearly white inside. He added a little olive oil and a dab of fresh mozzarella to each one. Then he cooked them in their shells until the cheese melted.

Down the beach, I could see a little body peek out from under the navy-blue Lodge umbrella. A few moments later, I heard a squeaky voice at my elbow. "What's that?" It was a small Lodge mouse, about my age. She was staring at the bubbling clams on our small fire.

Grandfather offered her a taste. She blew on it to cool it and took it in her mouth. Her eyes lit up with pleasure. "Good!" she said. "More, please!"

Just then her mother called out sharply down the beach, "Priscilla Peabody Lodge! Spit that out! That's filthy!"

Priscilla scampered back under the navy-blue umbrella, never to poke her head out again.

Grandfather saw my tears before they spilled from my eyes. "That lovely young mouse, wasn't she lucky? Born with a silver spoon in her mouth, and all those navy-blue umbrellas to protect her from the sun."

With envy in my eyes, I agreed that Priscilla Lodge was about as lucky as a mouse could get. I bit into the warm mozzarella clam, which made me feel a little bit better.

To cheer me up, after we finished our clams, Grandfather bought me a lemon-ice gelato at his friend Tonio's on the Revere Beach boardwalk.

After that we walked, Grandfather and I, hopping over the hot sand and down to where the tide lapped in and sandpipers skimmed for mole crabs in the lacey wavelets. And we looked for shells along the tide line as we always did.

"Do you see, my little biscotti," said Grandfather, "how Miss Priscilla Lodge's mother keeps her from venturing very far? Sheltered under that big blue umbrella, she may never discover Tonio's gelato, or taste fresh mozzarella on a clam again, or be allowed to talk to a gerbil. She is learning to be afraid of anything that is outside her own world."

Grandfather glanced down at me to see if I understood. I looked back at the fancy umbrellas, far away down the beach now.

"So who is the lucky one, do you think?" he asked.

I would never again look at the Lodges, Lowells, or Cabots with envy or shame.

11

We ended our walk at the streetcar stop. I slept with my sandy head in Grandfather's lap all the way back to Boston.

Chapter Two

When he was a young mouse, Grandfather came to Boston, from Naples, Italy, on the steamship *Leonardo da Vinci*. He stowed away in a coil of rope under a cleat, with only an inch square of wool blanket to keep him warm.

A single small lump of polenta kept him from starving. When he arrived in the port of Boston, he hopped into a box of dried cod.

The box of cod was delivered to Salvadore's
Spaghetti House in the city's North End,
and there Grandfather stayed.

In no time, he opened his own restaurant in the attic of Salvadore's, featuring daily specials from the kitchen downstairs. Grandfather's customers were mostly other mice from Italy. The restaurant was spotlessly clean, did not serve rats, and boasted the best southern Italian cooking in the city of Boston.

Grandfather worked hard for many years, and all that time he lived in a forgotten pine cupboard at the back of Salvadore's attic.

There he hung his few clothes and pasted pictures from the newspapers and letters he received from home.

As Salvadore's fame grew, so did
Grandfather's. He saved his money under
his mattress. He spent wisely, wore spats
with mother-of-pearl buttons, and combed
his silver ears and whiskers just so.

One day he fell in love with a small mouse the color of acorns. Her name was Jennie. He bought a bed and a table to go with his cupboard and said, "I am ready to be married."

Grandfather married his Jennie in the belfry of Holy Cross Cathedral on Washington Street.

Chapter Three

I was named for my grandmother, but I never had the chance to know her. By the time I came into this world, Grandmother Jennie was gone and Grandfather was already an old mouse. Eventually, he turned the running of the restaurant over to my mother and father, and began to look after me instead.

My parents worked late into the night, so it was Grandfather who spooned warm milk over my evening pudding. It was his hand that showed me how to button my buttons and how to draw *J* for *Jenny*. Into Grandfather's vest pocket went my first tooth, and to the ticking of his pocket watch I slept.

When I was old enough to go walking, Grandfather took me to the Italian cafés where his friends sat over cups of *cappolatte anisetto,* played cards, and gave me bits of biscotti dipped in coffee cream. I followed him everywhere through the city. I never lost sight of the waxed whiskers that stood straight out from his face, and I kept one eye on the silver ears that flicked with pride. The walking stick that he twirled, and sometimes

spun in the air, was never out of my view.

In that way I learned Boston. I learned all the mice in the city and what they did to make a living. Grandfather tipped his hat to Senator Lodge himself and to the Cabot nursemaids, the fried-seed vendor, and the poorest rat who swept the sewers. Grandfather said hello to the world. I learned to say hello, too, in that way that made the world smile back.

When I grew to be a young lady, Grandfather took me to the shops. A little known fact is that riddling the back storage rooms and air shafts of Jordan Marsh and Filene's department stores are hundreds of specialty boutiques, all run by mice for mice. There the latest fashions from Paris and Milan are copied exactly from the downstairs models. They are painstakingly sewn from snippets of silk and organza, stolen from the main racks at night.

"You may be the child of humble cooks," Grandfather said to me, "but you must always hold your head high, Jenny, and your whiskers straight as arrows."

So we went into the most expensive

and exclusive of the boutiques, Chanel
Souris. There I tried on every outfit and
modeled them for Grandfather. He sat
patiently, leaning on his mother-of-pearl–
tipped walking stick and examining the
tailoring carefully, as if we could have
afforded them.

"No," said Grandfather. "Too frou-frou!" or "I don't think it's quite your style." In the end we hung everything neatly back on its hangers and bought nothing.

"It is important," said Grandfather, "that you are able to go anywhere and say to the richest girl, 'Oh, I tried on those shoes last week. They look much better on you!'"

It was Grandfather who taught me the names of all the shells: luck shells, boat shells, comb shells, winkles, and the rare queen's teacup, which washes up only once in a blue moon.

"Queen's teacups have real gold in them," said Grandfather, but we only ever found bits of broken ones.

"Is there a real queen somewhere, Grandfather, who drinks from a queen's teacup?" I asked.

Grandfather answered. "Yes, a queen who lives in the cold northern sea. Many years ago a huge ship called the *Titanic* sank like a stone off the coast of Iceland. Hundreds of mice drowned. But one lucky mouse managed to crawl into a lantern bobbing on the surface. There was enough oxygen in it to last several hours, enough warmth so he did not freeze.

"From inside this glass bubble, he spied a kingdom under the icebergs. It belonged to one of the northern queens. Her jewel room was lit up with Saint Elmo's fire. In it were shells of the most amazing kind: pearl-lined cockles, emerald luck shells, and scallops speckled with gold. The queen's crown was there, too, set with sapphire winkles, and an entire set of gold queen's teacups was on display. He counted twenty-four with saucers."

"Did he go into the castle, Grandfather?"

"No. He didn't dare open the lantern door to take a souvenir. He would have drowned, or frozen, or both."

"What happened to him then?" I asked anxiously.

"There was a sudden yank on the lantern from above. The lantern was attached to a rope, and the rope was held by a sailor. In a moment the mouse and the lantern were aboard the rescue ship, *Carpathia*."

On Revere Beach, Grandfather and I watched a child's sandcastle melt into the tide.

"So the queen's teacups, if we are to find any, must travel all the way from the icy northern sea?" I asked in wonder.

"That's right," said Grandfather, "which is why they are so rare."

I tried to be as sharp-eyed a shell spotter as the old mouse who held my hand. But his eye was keener than mine. He always saw the glint of gold in the sand that I missed.

"Someday, Jenny," said Grandfather, "you will find a whole and perfect queen's teacup shell."

"Do you think so?" I asked.

"I know you will!" said Grandfather. "And when you do, it will be more precious and beautiful than anything in the whole Lodge mansion."

We went home then, hiding in the luggage bin of the Number 5 Revere Beach trolley.

Chapter Four

And then Grandfather was all of a sudden gone one day, never to come back. I had not understood that sometimes those we love are here on earth only a short time.

Hundreds of Boston mice came to Grandfather's funeral in the belfry of the cathedral. Even the Lodge mice came to pay respects, since Senator Lodge's favorite restaurant turned out to be Salvadore's.

I did nothing but walk in circles, crying, for days. My mother grew worried. My father tried to feed me up on veal parmesan. They closed the restaurant for the weekend and took me on a ferryboat to Martha's Vineyard. Nothing worked.

One day, crossing Boston Common in the mist, I spied Grandfather's tilted whiskers. *Impossible!* I told myself. I had seen Grandfather, cold as stone, in the matchbox coffin at his wake. I had placed a buttercup on his lapel before they closed up the box and put him in the ground.

No matter, I followed those whiskers through the crowds by the swan boats, my heart hammering. *It can't be him,* I told myself, but the pull to follow was as irresistible as the current of the sea. "Tilted Whiskers" sat down on a bench. But when I ran around to face him, it was not Grandfather at all.

It was someone else with the same whiskers. I went home and ate my spaghetti Milanese as if it were lead pellets.

After that, I began to see him everywhere. One day my mother sent me out to Kennedy's Dairy to steal a tablespoon of butter from the storage room. When I came out of Kennedy's, butter lump in a string bag, I spotted a pair of silver ears gleaming in the afternoon sun.

"Grandfather!" I called. The mouse didn't hear me. He and his silver ears vanished behind Faneuil Hall. I followed. He was headed for Boston Harbor.

I ran to catch up and saw him leap from an oily bollard to the deck of a lobster boat.

"Grandfather!" I called again, and jumped onto the deck of the lobster boat.

But it wasn't Grandfather. It wasn't even a mouse. It was only a sailor rat who'd spiffed up his ears with Brylcreem.

I stopped abruptly and slipped on a mackerel skin. I skittered, then fell into the filthy water between two mountainous clanging, banging ships.

I was pulled from the drink on a banana peel by the Harbor Patrol, all sleek Boston water voles. Chattering through pointed yellow teeth, they took me back to my parents.

My father and mother were beside themselves with worry. "No more following Grandfather," they said. "You cannot find him, Jenny. Grandfather is gone."

I did not try again. Instead I made a little bed for myself in Grandfather's old wardrobe. I slept under his favorite jackets, which still smelled of him, and read his newspaper stories and letters from home, pasted so long ago on the inside walls.

Chapter Five

Fall turned early to winter. I was busy in the kitchen that year. My mother showed me how to make a floating island as light as an angel's wing. My father taught me the secrets of tortellini.

Late as always, spring came to Boston in May. My mother served my own lasagna *puttanesca* to the customers. It was so popular that they included it as "Lasagna Jenny" on the regular menu.

My parents closed the restaurant for
the July Fourth holiday. We took the trolley
to Tonio's for ice cream.

"I miss the old fellow," said Tonio, and
he served us chocolate gelato with whipped
cream, Grandfather's favorite.

While I stared at the floor, Mother and Father and Tonio exchanged stories. Through the crowd of customers' feet, I spotted a walking stick with a mother-of-pearl tip! I jumped up. My parents and Tonio did not notice.

I followed the tap-tapping stick out the door, over the boardwalk, and to the beach. The figure kept just ahead of me, disappearing behind a rock and then a hill of sand.

"Stop!" I shouted, puffing. "Grandfather! Stop!"

On enormous Revere Beach, I looked for him. Running, running, running along the wet strand near the waves, the foam lapping at my tail, I called Grandfather's name. The sun bounced off the water in a thousand mirrors, and I had to squint. All I could make out were dots of light, sandpiper footprints, and burping clam holes. Whoever it was with the walking stick had vanished.

At the end of the beach, the white fringe of the deep-blue Lodge umbrella fluttered in the breeze.

Suddenly, a wave swamped me and pulled me out into the sea. Just as suddenly, I felt myself being lifted by a pair of unseen arms, and I was deposited back onto the edge of the beach and into a melting sand castle.

In a crenellated tower, I caught my breath for several minutes. Whoever had made the castle had decorated it with delicately placed shells. There were boat shells and double luck shells, and winkles and comb shells.

But, joy of joys — into the arch over the seaweed portcullis were embedded four perfect gold queen's teacups! I had never seen even a single whole one before. I removed the shells carefully and took them home.

I have never seen Grandfather's silver ears or tilted whiskers again, but my heart is at peace. Whenever I miss him, I only have to take the trolley to Revere Beach and walk out along the edge of the sea behind Tonio's. There, in the sun and the ocean wind, Grandfather always says hello to me in shells.